MICHAEL J. ROS

A Thanksgiving Wish

paintings by

JOHN THOMPSON

SCHOLASTIC INC.

New York Toronto London Auckland Sydney
Mexico City New Delhi Hong Kong

For the grandmothers we never stop remembering

— M. J. R.

For my grandmother, Margaret; my mother, Dorothy;

my wife, Darren; and my sisters-in-law, Kathy and Lauren —

thank you for all the wonderful Thanksgivings

— J. M. T.

This book was originally published in hardcover by the Blue Sky Press in 1999.

ISBN 0-590-25564-9

12 11 10 9 8 7 6 5 4 3 2 1   0 1 2 3 4 5/0

Printed in the United States of America   14

Designed by Kathleen Westray

First Scholastic paperback printing, October 2000

ONCE A YEAR, ever since Amanda knew the word
Thanksgiving, her family would travel to her grandmother Bubbe's house
for the holiday. Even more than Chanukah or Passover or the other
Jewish holidays that Bubbe loved to share with her family, Thanksgiving
had always been Bubbe's special holiday.

At sunup, Amanda, her older sisters Caroline and Betsy, her mother,
and her father all began the drive across three states to join her aunts,
uncles, and cousins at the house where Bubbe's three children had
been born. Bubbe often visited them, but it was only once a year that
Amanda and her cousins, all of them older, gathered at their
grandmother's house.

The whole month of November, Bubbe prepared the exact same meal that she had cooked for…well, it was hard to remember, but for at least as many years as Amanda's mother could remember. Without the slightest help from anyone, not even from Grandpa when he was alive, Bubbe cooked every one of the dishes they'd pass from dining room to kitchen to living room.

Even with everyone squishing together, they needed three tables. Bubbe would always have known of someone's relative who had nowhere to spend the holiday, and she would set an extra place.

Bubbe cooked one holiday dish each day—say, her famous maple applesauce—alongside whatever else she was cooking for her own

dinner or lunch. No single part of her Thanksgiving dinner was less than a family favorite: a tom turkey so heavy that Bubbe recruited the neighbor's son to lift it in and out of the oven; a stuffing made from her own braided challah; the tzimmes of prunes and apricots that stewed all day with lemons and both kinds of potatoes; the chicken soup with matzo balls so light they floated; snowflake rolls; gelatin molds with ten different layers that took days to make; a trout-shaped cranberry mold; honey cakes; and of course enough pumpkin pies for each family to take one home.

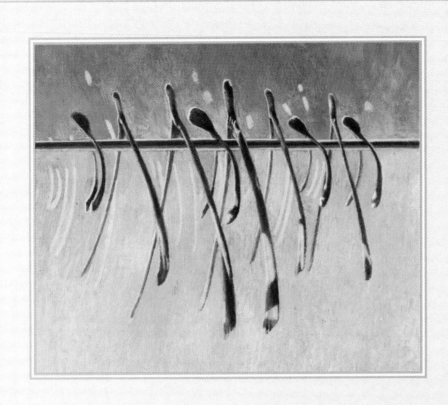

But for Amanda, the best part of the visit came right before bed: her Thanksgiving wishbone. All year long, her grandmother saved the wishbones from every sort of bird she cooked. Picked clean and washed, they dried along the curtain rod above the sink—a whole row of future wishes awaiting the arrival of her grandchildren. Somehow, even after Grandpa died and she only had herself and the occasional stray cat to feed, Bubbe's supply of wishbones was large enough so that every grandchild could have one wish each night during the Thanksgiving visit.

"What size wish do you have tonight?" Bubbe would ask, sitting on the edge of Amanda's bed. In her hand lay three wishbones: a big tom turkey wishbone, a medium-sized wishbone from a roasting chicken, and a third wishbone from a little game hen.

When Amanda's father's company considered moving them all far away, or when their cat, Augustine, hadn't found its way home after a week of being lost, Amanda chose a tom turkey bone. The chicken wishbone seemed right for starting piano lessons and hoping that Lorraine Caldwell would quit calling her names at school. Amanda picked the littlest bones for wishes like her first pair of ice skates—and a ton of snow that might close school so she could use them.

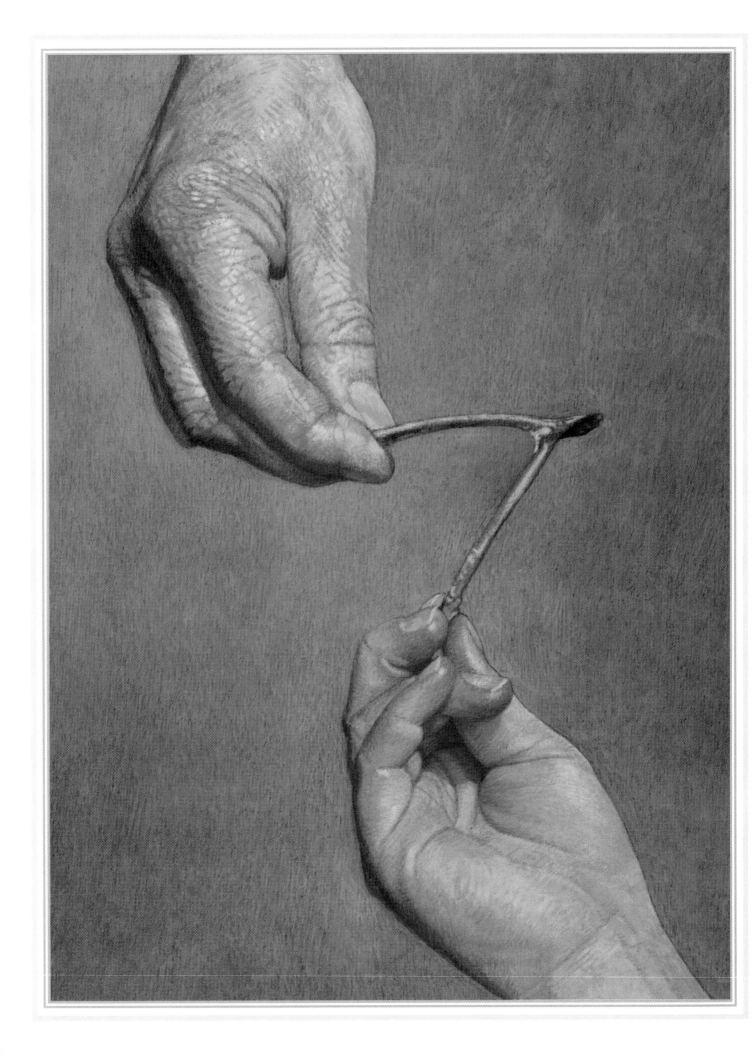

"Ready? Hold tight," Bubbe would say. "One…two…three…snap!"

Whoever held the largest piece of the wishbone would have one wish granted—as long as the wish was never mentioned to anyone else.

The Thanksgiving before Bubbe died, as unexpectedly as anything you want to live forever dies, Amanda asked her a question. "Bubbe, I've always wondered: What are you wishing for tonight? I know we're not supposed to tell, but maybe…well, can you tell me what you wished for last year?"

Her grandmother held out the wishbone for Amanda to grab, and said, "Tonight? Last year? I'm wishing for the same thing I wish for every time."

"And what's that?" Amanda asked.

Bubbe paused, as if she thought Amanda might guess the answer, and then replied, "One…two…three…snap!" as if that were the answer itself.

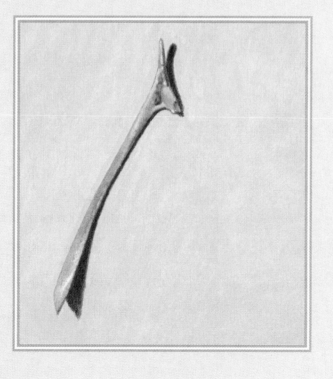

And so for the first Thanksgiving without Bubbe, Amanda's family invited everyone to their new house—really, it was an *old* house with three floors and lots of rooms that needed every sort of fix-up and repair. But the dining room would be spacious enough to hold everybody around one table. So Thanksgiving would be their out-of-town relations' first visit.

In the days before Thanksgiving, when Bubbe would have been cooking and cooking, Amanda began missing her grandmother more and more.

"You never stop missing someone, Mandi," her father said one night as he tucked her into bed. "You sort of forget how much you miss them until something—like Thanksgiving—reminds you again. And then it's missing them, and it's sadness all over again, until some other happier thing—like the fact that all your cousins are coming tomorrow—makes you forget again."

But the next afternoon, preparing stuffing alongside her mother and sisters, Mandi could tell that they were, all of them, having a hard time forgetting about Bubbe.

"I know. Let's go through Bubbe's recipe file—I have it downstairs," Amanda's mother said. "Maybe we'll find out how to make everything that Bubbe usually made, and we'll cook up her perfect Thanksgiving dinner for everyone!"

"Sounds delicious," Amanda said.

"Sounds hard," her sister Betsy said. "She never cooked everything in one day."

All night, Amanda's entire family—even her father, who never made more than frozen orange juice—grated, sliced, measured, mixed, stirred, and chopped, readying each of Bubbe's traditional favorites to be cooked the next day.

Thanksgiving morning, the rain poured down. It was one of those dark, gray days when the lamppost never turns off. Right after breakfast, the cooking marathon began again: Amanda herself helped peel potatoes for the tzimmes, steam pumpkins for the pie, and knead dough for the snowflake rolls.

Aunt Honey and Uncle Paul arrived with their four children before noon, and Aunt Sonny arrived with her four children an hour later. All of them were soaked, or at least damp, from the chilly rain.

"Dinner's going to be a little late," Amanda's mother told her houseful of guests, "even though the other chefs and I have been working full-time since yesterday."

In the meantime, the aunts stationed themselves at each of the kitchen appliances (as well as the dryer, spinning the rain-drenched clothes). The fathers built a fire and gathered at the TV. The girls helped their cousins settle into the giant third-floor attic, where they all were going to sleep. But in every part of the busy house, the talk turned to Bubbe, as if Thanksgiving couldn't begin without her. Maybe all the cooking smells brought her to mind: lemony, yeasty, mapley, oniony. A Bubbe scent rose from nearly every pot and pan in the house.

And then, right in the middle of all this busyness, the lights went out. The fan above the stove stopped whirring. The TV went black. The tzimmes quit its bubbling, the thumping of the dryer ceased—everything stopped.

"Hey, what happened?"

"Who turned out the lights?"

"Uh-oh…"

"The lightning must have cut off the electricity!" Amanda's mother cried.

"But I didn't see lightning," Amanda called back. "And I didn't hear thunder, either."

"She's right. All the neighbors have power," Aunt Honey observed from the window.

"I'll get the candles," Amanda's father said on his way to the basement.

Even though it was only three in the afternoon, the rain clouds made it look like evening.

"Oh, this is just great," Aunt Sonny said. "Raw turkey, hard potatoes, cold soup, soupy pies. Well, I suppose we can have crackers and applesauce for dinner, right?"

"We need more than candles," her father announced from the top of the basement stairs. "We've blown the fuses. Between the stove, the two ovens, the microwave, the dishwasher, the dryer, and all these lights, we overloaded the old electrical system. I'm afraid it's candles until the hardware store opens tomorrow."

"But Thanksgiving dinner!" Amanda's mother exclaimed.

"Don't get upset. We'll figure out something," Aunt Honey offered. "If only we had a whole month to cook, like Bubbe..."

But before anyone could speak, a knock was heard at the side door.
Amanda opened the door to find an elderly woman bundled in a

raincoat, clutching a small
umbrella. "I saw that your
lights went out. Is everything
all right? I'm Betty Yee. That's
my house across the alley.
You might need this," she
said, holding out an enormous
flashlight.

"Mom," Amanda called,
"it's our neighbor, Mrs. Yee."

With all the unpacking,
painting, and new schoolwork, Amanda's family hadn't really met their
neighbors. Her parents, clearly embarrassed by this, hurried to the door.

"Oh, how kind of you. Come in—dry off. We've blown the fuses,
cooking everything at once!"

Mrs. Yee stepped inside and switched on her flashlight. Its beam
shined across the pale turkey, the unbaked pies, the counters lined with
all the raw, uncooked, and cold parts of dinner.

"Now, listen to me. I have nothing cooking at my house," Mrs. Yee
told them, "so please come cook it there."

"Oh, no, we couldn't dream of imposing on your holiday plans," said
Amanda's father.

"But I have no plans. I celebrated with some friends much earlier.
Come. Let's just carry it all across the alley. You'll finish cooking there."

Amanda's parents offered more polite refusals, but Mrs. Yee insisted.
And no one else offered any other possibilities.

Out into the rain, Amanda's family paraded in pairs. Some carried covered dishes, and others held up umbrellas and draped plastic tablecloths over their heads.

Unfortunately, the tom turkey was too big for Mrs. Yee's oven. The giant pot of chicken soup fit across two of her stove's burners, but as for a microwave or an electric mixer...

"Well, at least start the pies," Aunt Honey suggested. "And I'll come back and bake the snowflake rolls."

"Don't worry, I just thought of the perfect solution," Mrs. Yee said. "I'm pet-sitting for the Reynolds family next door. They're all in New York now, except for their sleepy old dog—and he's probably not using their oven. They have an extra-modern kitchen!"

Armistead, the bearded collie, couldn't have been happier to have this Thanksgiving company.

Although the turkey fit into the Reynolds' oven, no one could figure out how to program the temperature. "I think it's a convection oven," Amanda's mother guessed. "It's too technical for this old bird!" So this time, they left a couple of other dishes to heat in the Reynolds' microwave (which was easy enough to work) and headed toward the door, ready to give up the turkey and stuffing.

"Not so fast! Now, it's over to the Ashers'," Mrs. Yee announced, pointing across the block to the house two doors away from Amanda's. "They ate around noon, too, I think. I noticed all the cars."

Sure enough, Mrs. Asher welcomed her new neighbors and their turkey into her house. She listened to the story of their Bubbe's legendary meal, and she led Amanda's father straight to her oven. "And I happen to be an expert at basting, so go enjoy your company, and I'll call you when it's about ready."

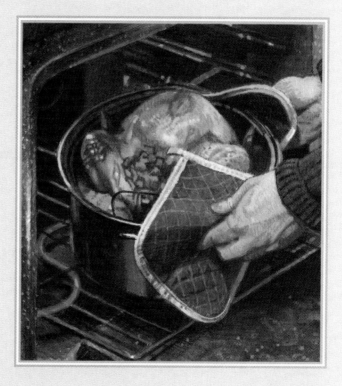

Amazingly, Bubbe's complete Thanksgiving dinner would be served after all—with Amanda and Aunt Honey cooking at Mrs. Yee's house, Caroline and Aunt Sonny at the Ashers', Betsy and her mother (and Armistead) at the Reynolds'—while all the husbands and cousins waited in the candlelit dark of the new house.

But it was hard to cook in other people's kitchens. And it was even harder to cook things that they had never before attempted. In each of the three kitchens, Bubbe's children and grandchildren were wondering if this really had been such a good idea.

Much later, through the downpour, the family paraded back to Amanda's house with their potholders and umbrellas and covered dishes. This time Mrs. Yee couldn't refuse their offer, and Amanda brought Armistead, who, she decided, shouldn't spend the holiday alone.

"We tried our very, very best to recreate all of Mom's dishes," Amanda's mother began. "But, well, as you know, not everything went as planned."

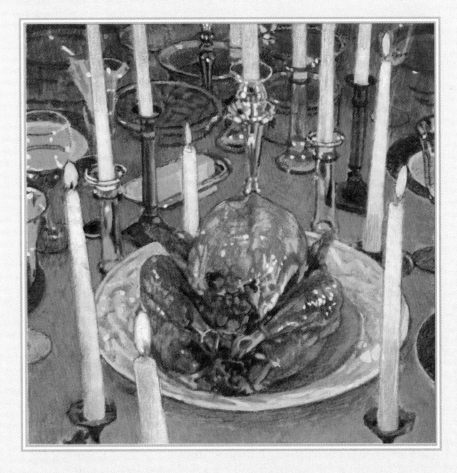

"It all looks wonderful," Uncle Paul said. "She couldn't have done better."

"Well, I know her gravy was never lumpy," Amanda's mother admitted.

But because everyone was tired and famished, they forgot to compare each dish with their memories of Bubbe's cooking. There in the dark, surrounded by windowsills lined with candles, all of Bubbe's children, grandchildren, and last-minute guests managed all the laughter, and the storytelling, and the second helpings that they had shared every other Thanksgiving around Bubbe's table.

Just as everyone began to lean back in their chairs, so full and satisfied, and just as the serving plates were passed one more time in case somebody couldn't resist another spoonful of something, Amanda started to cry.

"What's wrong, Mandi?" her father asked.

All eyes in the room looked to Amanda as she pointed to the wishbone on the platter Aunt Sonny was holding.

"There's only one bone for wishing on. No one saved them up for all us little kids," she said.

Both of Amanda's parents came to her side, but not before Uncle Paul could say, "Since you're the youngest of all the grandchildren, you should make the wish. You probably got the fewest wishbones of anyone here, right?"

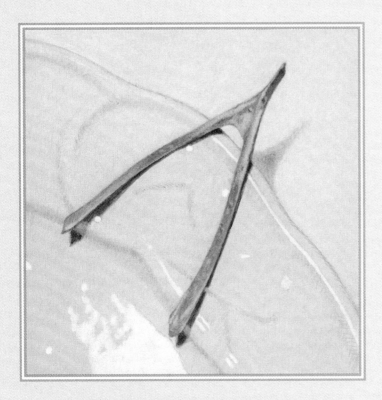

While no one disagreed with the suggestion, Amanda's tears didn't stop. She managed to say, "But there's no grandma to wish with."

For the longest moment, no one knew what to do or say. A few knives and forks were slid across the mostly empty plates. The rain suddenly seemed especially loud against the panes. But then, from among the ring of chairs shoved arm to arm around the table, Mrs. Yee asked, "I wonder if I could be the grandmother—I mean, I am one, you know. Eight grandchildren, but they're in Washington, D.C."

Amanda looked at her mother and her father, but they merely returned her gaze, as if only Amanda knew the answer. Finally, she reached for the wishbone and looked over to Mrs. Yee.

"We'd all be honored," Amanda's father replied.

"You'll have to tell me what to do," Mrs. Yee said, reaching toward Amanda.

"Whoever breaks off the biggest half gets to make a wish," Amanda explained. "But you can't tell what the wish is, or it might not come true."

"That sounds fair," said Mrs. Yee.

"Oh, and since this is a big wishbone, you're allowed to make a big wish," Amanda said. "Now, press your thumb here, and on the count of three, pull." All the eyes in the room watched the wishbone as if everyone were joining in to make the same enormous wish. "One… two…three." *Snap!*

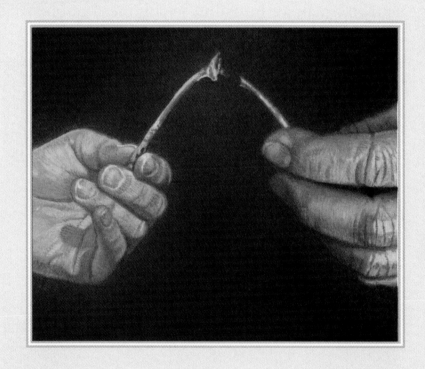

"Oh, well," sighed Mrs. Yee, holding her small splinter in the air. "I'm afraid I've lost."

A smile returned to Amanda's face, but the tracks of tears still shone on her cheeks. "You know what I wished for?" she asked of no one in particular.

"Amanda! You're not supposed to tell," her sister Betsy barked.

"Well, I can say this one, because it's the kind that can't come true. Anyway, I wish Bubbe were here."

"Oh, Amanda," her father said, "we all wish that. Don't we, everyone?" And, indeed, everyone at the table mumbled yes, almost at the same time.

Her mother said, "Make another wish, sweetheart. One that really might come true."

"But I can't think of what to wish for."

"Well, maybe since we're all thinking about Bubbe now," Amanda's mother said, "she wouldn't mind if I told her secret. Do you know what wish Bubbe made each time she broke a wishbone with each of you?"

"No, tell us. She wouldn't tell, and I even asked one time," Amanda said, looking to each of her sisters and cousins to see if they knew.

Amanda's mother stood tall again, and pressed her thumbs together, as if to break an invisible wishbone. "Bubbe made the same wish every

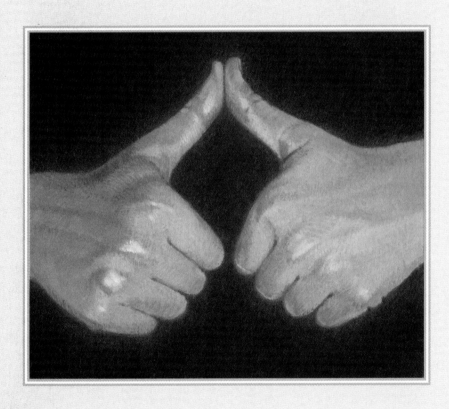

time. She wished for you to break off the bigger piece."

"But why?" Amanda asked. "She wanted to lose?"

"Don't you see? Because her one wish was to have your wishes come true."

Amanda thought about that a long time. Long enough for some of her relatives to start talking again and for the rain to quiet down. Long enough for Armistead to nose his way beside Amanda's chair to check for a dropped chunk of stuffing. Long enough for Mrs. Yee to begin a story about a Thanksgiving in San Francisco, where she used to live.

"Now I know my wish," Amanda announced at last, and she lifted her wishbone with its flat tip pointing up like a make-believe candle and flame. "But I'm not telling. It's a secret between Bubbe and me."

And though Amanda never did tell anyone her wish, every year after that, her family, Aunt Honey's and Aunt Sonny's families, and even Mrs. Yee—who became a good friend—each saved up a year of wishbones and made their wishes on Thanksgiving night.